The Wild Girl

For Mary, Jane and Jo

THE WILD GIRL
A RED FOX BOOK 978 0 099 45148 8 (from January 2007)
0 099 45148 4

First published in Great Britain by Jonathan Cape, an imprint of Random House Children's Books

Jonathan Cape edition published 2005
Red Fox edition published 2006
1 3 5 7 9 10 8 6 4 2

Red Fox Books are published by Random House Children's Books, 61–63 Uxbridge Road, London W5 5SA,
a division of The Random House Group Ltd, in Australia by Random House Australia (Pty) Ltd,
20 Alfred Street, Milsons Point, Sydney, NSW 2061, Australia, in New Zealand by Random House New Zealand Ltd,
18 Poland Road, Glenfield, Auckland 10, New Zealand, in South Africa by Random House (Pty) Ltd,
Isle of Houghton, Corner Boundary Road & Carse O'Gowrie, Houghton 2198, South Africa
and in India by Random House India PVT Ltd, 301 World Trade Tower,
Hotel Intercontinental Grand Complex, Barakhamba Lane, New Delhi 110001, India
THE RANDOM HOUSE GROUP Limited Reg. No. 954009
www.kidsatrandomhouse.co.uk

A CIP catalogue record for this book is available from the British Library
Printed in Singapore

The Wild Girl

Chris Wormell

RED FOX

This is the story of a little girl and a small brown dog who lived all alone in the wilderness. The little girl had no one to brush her hair, or wash her face, or tie her shoelaces like you do. So her hair was a terrible mess and her face quite grubby. She had no shoelaces to tie because she had no shoes – but her feet had tough soles that were quite used to stepping on sharp stones, so she didn't need them.

The small brown dog had fleas, and I expect the little girl did too.

The little girl never went to school, because of course there were no schools in the wilderness. She had to learn things for herself. The small brown dog learnt too.

There were no shops,
so they couldn't buy food.
They had to hunt for it.

Sometimes they
caught trout . . .

. . . and cooked them over a little fire of twigs.

Sometimes they gathered
berries and roots.

They even ate insects.

They lived in a cave,
high up on the side of a
mountain. From there they
could look out and see far,
far away, almost to the edge
of the world. And in all the
wide wilderness, the little girl
never once saw the smoke
of another fire curling up
into the sky.

Sometimes she called out,
but never heard a reply, save for the
echo of her own voice, calling back
from the far mountaintops.

When the small brown dog barked,
he was puzzled – there seemed to be
lots of other dogs all around the mountains,
but he could never see any of them.

On warm summer nights, the little girl and the
small brown dog slept out under the stars.

Then, in the autumn, they gathered dry bracken and made a big nest at the back of the cave. It was cosy and snug, and mostly it was warm.

But in the coldest weather they often kept a fire burning through the night.

One winter's day, the little girl and the
small brown dog were collecting firewood,
when they came upon tracks in the snow.
Big tracks.
Bear tracks.
Tracks heading towards the cave.

They followed the tracks,
and when they reached the
cave, the small brown dog
began to growl.

But the bear had gone.

Inside, they found the bracken nest was squashed flat.

The small brown dog began to growl again.

He could smell bear.

They were certain the bear would come back.

And it did . . .

That night there was a
blizzard. The wind howled
and the snow began to pile
up in drifts outside the cave.
And as the little girl and the small
brown dog watched the storm, they
saw a great, dark shape coming up the
mountainside.

Soon the shape filled the mouth
of the cave . . .

The bear would have come right in, but the
little girl and the small brown dog barred
the way. This was their cave, and no one
could take it from them – not even a
big bad bear. They would fight for it!

The bear could easily have brushed
them aside with a paw, but it
didn't. It looked down at
them with strange, sad
eyes, then turned
and left the cave.

The small brown dog barked and the little girl cried out in triumph,
and threw a snowball after the bad old bear as it disappeared
into the stormy night.

Then they heard a
sound from the
cave behind
them . . .

. . . and creeping out from the
darkest corner, behind the
squashed bracken nest,
came a tiny bear cub.

The little girl realized that the bear was not a bad
bear after all, just a mother bear looking for her cub.

She dropped her spear and ran out into the blizzard,
calling after the mother bear.

But she was gone, and the falling snow
had covered her tracks.

After a while, it stopped snowing. The wind broke up the clouds and
the moon shone down on the wide, lonely wilderness.

There was no sign of the mother bear.

The little girl turned and trudged back up to the cave.

The snow had drifted deep, too deep for short legs,
and she carried the small brown dog under one arm
and the tiny cub under the other.

And who should they find sitting waiting
by the cave but the mother bear.

That winter, the cave high up on the mountainside was the snuggest, warmest place in all the wide wilderness.

But by the spring, they all had fleas!